# King of the Classroom

**DERRICK BARNES**

illustrated by
**VANESSA BRANTLEY-NEWTON**

Scallywag Press Ltd
LONDON

First published in Great Britain in 2020 by Scallywag Press Ltd,
10 Sutherland Row, London SW1V 4JT

Published by arrangement with Nancy Paulsen Books, an imprint of Penguin Young Readers Group,
a division of Penguin Random House LLC

Printed on FSC paper in China by Toppan Leefung

001

British Library Cataloguing in Publication Data available

978-1-912650-36-1

To Prince Nnamdi Thelonius — my baby.  — D.B.

For All the Children of the world, I see you.  — V.B.-N.

A child must learn early to believe
that he is somebody worthwhile and
that he can do many praiseworthy
things. The child must have the love of
family and the protection they give in
order to LIVE and FLOURISH.

—Benjamin Mays

The morning sun blares through your window like a million brass trumpets.

It sits and shines behind your head— like a crown.

Mummy says that today, you are going to be King of the Classroom!

You'll use a golden brush to clean Ye Royal Toothlets.

You'll wash your own face with a cloth bearing the family crest.

You'll dress yourself neatly in handpicked garments from the far-off villages of Osh and Kosh. B'gosh! You'll be ready to reign!

"My baby is heading to school," Mummy will say during breakfast.

But you're not a "baby"—could a baby wolf down His Royal Breakfast the way you can?

I don't think so.

"You're growing up so fast," Daddy will say.
And he'll be right!

"I can't stay the same size forever, can I?" you'll
say. "One day, I'll be taller than you, Daddy, and
you'll be *my* little man."

Daddy will laugh, but you won't be joking.

Then a big yellow carriage will deliver you to a grand fortress.

As you walk up to the towering doors, you'll remember Mummy saying, "Hold your head high and greet everyone with a brilliant, beaming, majestic smile. For you are King of the Classroom."

Your teacher will welcome you with a warm smile and a friendly "Good morning."
She'll be delighted by how you recite your name with pride.

When you head to your royal seat, the kids at your Round Table will wave and say, "Hi!" as if they've been waiting for you all summer.

So you smile back, return the wave, and give them a cheerful, "Hi, everybody!"

The truth is, you couldn't wait to meet your Classroom Kingdom, either.

Your teacher will go over classroom rules, and you'll all discuss important matters such as shapes, the alphabet, and the never-ending mystery of numbers. She'll even read a book about trucks, trains, and tractors.

WHEW! It sounds like a lot, but you're King of the Classroom. Piece. Of. Cake.

You will show your bravery at playtime when you go up to one of your classmates and ask, "Marie, do you wanna play with me?"

Not only will she say yes, but she'll lead
the way in helping you save the kingdom
by battling a fire-breathing dragon!

When it's time for a snack, the boy sitting next to you will be missing dessert.

You'll have packed your favourite—chocolate pudding—with an extra cup just in case.

So you'll say to him, "Want a pudding, Howie?"

He'll say thanks, and you won't mind at all, because what could be cooler than sharing with new friends?

After a royal rest,

you'll arise to sing and dance
and bop to a rhythmic beat.

The day will be one you'll never forget.

At the end of it, your teacher will wish
you all a magnificent evening and bid
you farewell until dawn.

HOOL BUS

On your way back home, you'll think of all the things you can't wait to tell your parents.
"I made a bunch of new friends. My teacher is nice. And playtime is the best thing ever!"

And tomorrow, it will begin again—another day
as the charming, the wonderful, and the kind . . .

# King of the Classroom